Old Mother Hubbard

Old Mother Hubbard went to the cupboard
To fetch her poor dog a bone;
But the skeleton there said, "Hey! Don't you dare!
Leave all of my pieces alone!"

Sing a Song of Witches

Sing a song of witches, pocket full of sage,

Four and twenty blackbirds locked in a cage.

When the cage was opened, the birds took to the sky,

But before they flew away, they had a trick to try.

The witch was in the garden, picking thyme and rue,

Cackling as she dreamed of tasty blackbird stew.

She hobbled to her cauldron and mixed her herbs with care

When down came those blackbirds and pulled out her hair.

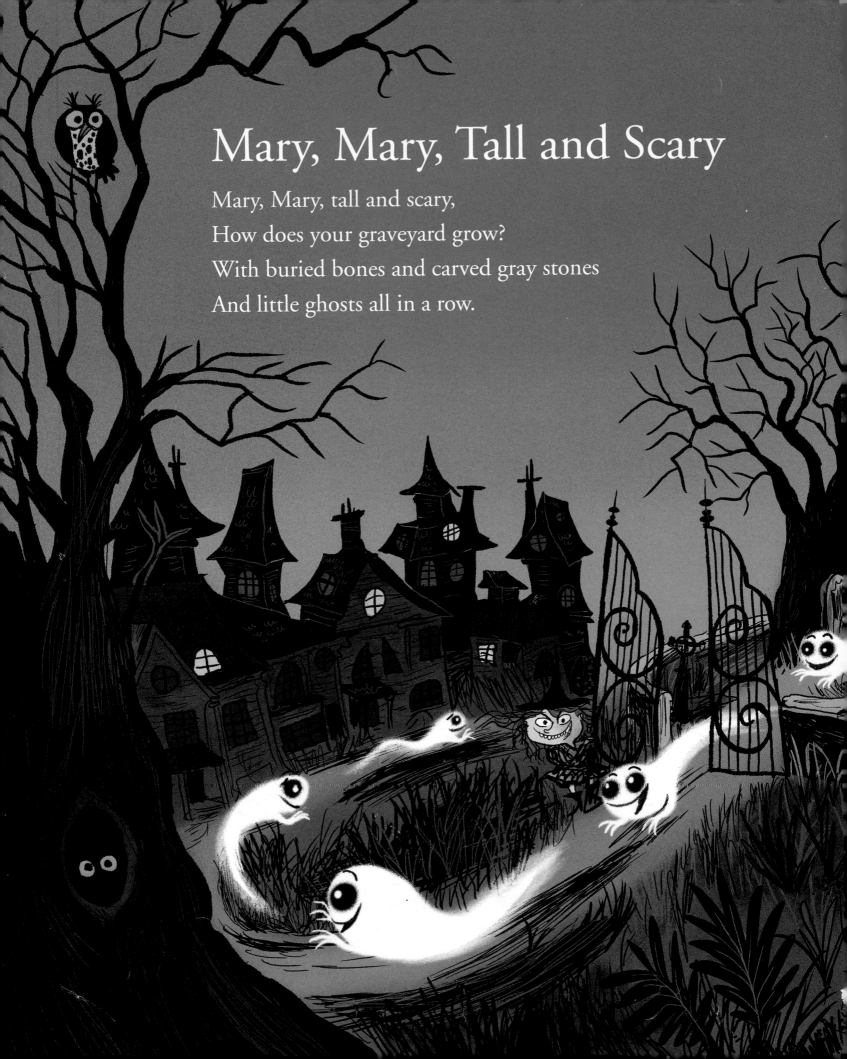

Mary, Mary, Tall and Scary

Mary, Mary, tall and scary,
How does your graveyard grow?
With buried bones and carved gray stones
And little ghosts all in a row.

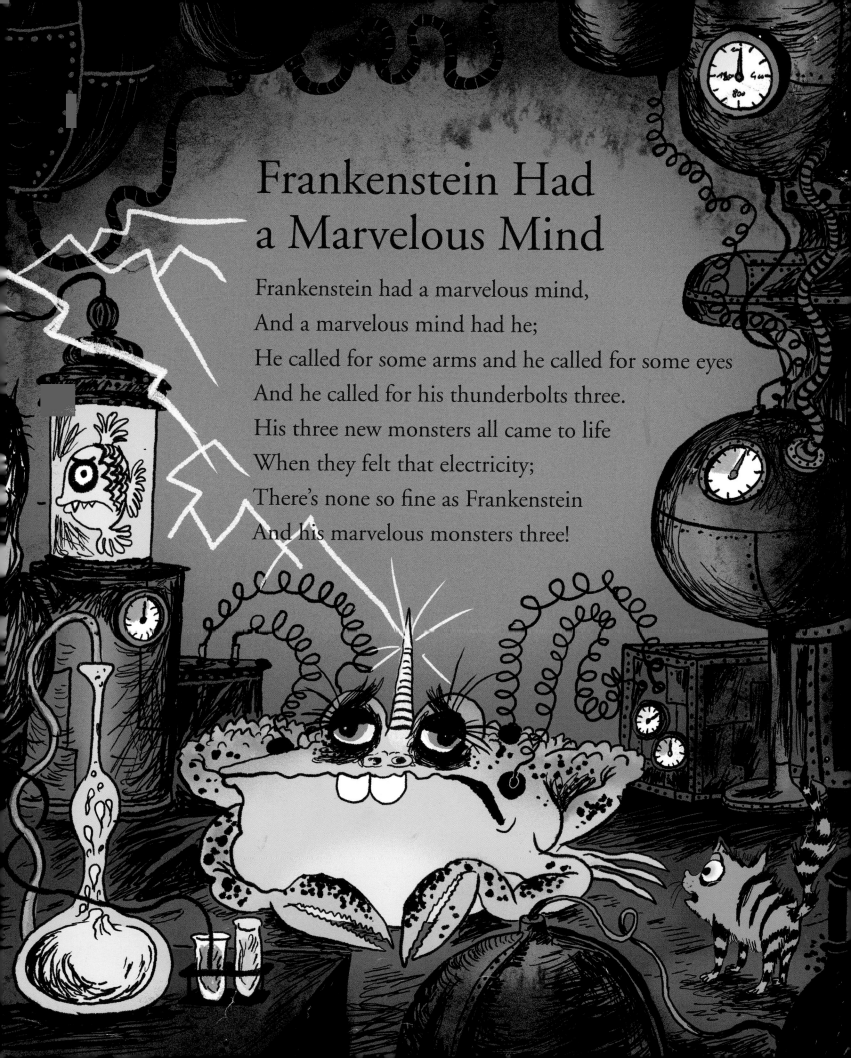

Frankenstein Had a Marvelous Mind

Frankenstein had a marvelous mind,

And a marvelous mind had he;

He called for some arms and he called for some eyes

And he called for his thunderbolts three.

His three new monsters all came to life

When they felt that electricity;

There's none so fine as Frankenstein

And his marvelous monsters three!

Little Boy Drac

Little boy Drac, come sound the call;

The bat's in the belfry, the rat's in the wall.

Where is the boy who looks after those creeps?

He's inside his coffin, fast asleep.

Will you wake him? No, not I;

My garlic breath will make him cry.

Twinkle, Twinkle, Lantern Jack

Twinkle, twinkle, lantern Jack,
Grinning orange against the black,
Crouched beneath the window light,
Like a watchman in the night.

Wee Willie Werewolf

Wee Willie Werewolf runs down the street,
Upstairs and downstairs on his clawed feet.
Growling at the window, howling to the skies,
"Are the monsters all in bed? The sun's about to rise!"

To my sweet little monsters: Billy, Liza, and the Pumpkin
—Rachel

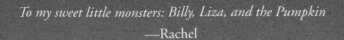

To my young godson Bartholomé and his cousin, Louis the nightmare's poet!
—Roland

Text Copyright © 2018 Rachel Kolar • Illustration Copyright © 2018 Roland Garrigue • Design Copyright © 2018 Sleeping Bear Press • All rights reserved. No part of this book may be reproduced in any manner without the express written consent of the publisher, except in the case of brief excerpts in critical reviews and articles. • All inquiries should be addressed to: **Sleeping Bear Press**™ • 2395 South Huron Parkway, Suite 200, Ann Arbor, MI 48104 • www.sleepingbearpress.com © Sleeping Bear Press • Printed and bound in the United States • 10 9 8 7 6 5 4 3 2 1 • Library of Congress Cataloging-in-Publication Data : Names: Kolar, Rachel, author. • Garrigue, Roland, 1979- illustrator. • Title: Mother Ghost : spooky rhymes for Halloween • written by Rachel Kolar ; illustrated by Roland Garrigue. • Other titles: Mother Goose. • Description: Ann Arbor, MI : Sleeping Bear Press, [2018] • Summary: An illustrated collection of thirteen gently spooky Mother Goose rhymes. • Identifiers: LCCN 2018014048 • ISBN 9781585363926 (alk. paper) Subjects: LCSH: Nursery rhymes. • Children's poetry. • CYAC: Nursery rhymes. • Halloween- Poetry. Classification: LCC PZ8.3 .K7535 Mot 2018 • DDC [E]-dc23 LC record available at https://lccn.loc.gov/2018014048